DECEMBER
STORIES I

IAN SANSOM

First published in 2018
by No Alibis Press

Printed and bound by TJ International, Padstow

A CIP record for this book
is available from the British Library

ISBN 978-1999882235

2 4 6 8 10 9 7 5 3 1

for Chris and Jaz

'Every idiot who goes about with Merry Christmas on his lips should be boiled with his own pudding and buried with a stake of holly through his heart.'

Charles Dickens, 'A Christmas Carol'

CONTENTS

Preface   xi

1 DECEMBER

2 DECEMBER

3 DECEMBER

4 DECEMBER

5 DECEMBER

6 DECEMBER

7 DECEMBER

8 DECEMBER

9 DECEMBER

10 DECEMBER

PREFACE

Good stories are never quite true, particularly at this time of year.

These stories are all as true as I can possibly make them.

I remember my grandmother seeing the snow on the lawn at my parents' house, the last Christmas she was alive, after several glasses of sherry and having cheated us all at cards, and her saying, 'Look! The green is all white.'

What can I say?

Look! The green is all white.

Ian Sansom
Co. Down

1 DECEMBER

It's All About the Wings

Our daughter is an angel. We have been asked to make wings. My wife asks me to make the wings.

It is a busy time of year at work.

I start with cardboard. I make cardboard wings from a cereal box. The wings are not big enough.

I use two cereal boxes.

My wife says the cereal box wings are not good enough. She emails me a link to a website that explains how to make wings using a wire base covered in fabric and decorated with glitter.

I delete the email and pretend I haven't received it.

It is late October. Then it is November. Then it is late November.

My wife asks how I am getting on with the wings.

I say I'm getting on fine.

It is the first week of December.

In the end we go with the cardboard. I get some bigger boxes from the supermarket and I use marker pens and some coloured paper, and some glitter.

One of our daughter's friends has wings made from sculpted foam, covered with feathers. Another girl has wings made of thousands of strips of coloured material, built on a wire frame attached to an old rucksack: the wingspan of her wings is at least six feet. Another girl—whose father is a plumber—has made Space Age wings from plastic piping sprayed silver and gold. My wife shows me the photographs on her phone.

'They are wings,' says my wife.

I agree that they are indeed wings.

'It's not about the wings though, is it,' I say.

'That,' says my wife, 'is what you don't understand. It's all about the wings.'

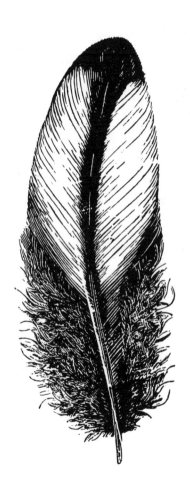

2 DECEMBER

Fort Lauderdale, Florida, Christmas 1979

My father had remarried, for the first time. She was American, the second wife, and there were four in total: my mother; then the American; then an Irish one; and then another American. But it was this one, the second wife, the first American, who really counted. Their marriage lasted little more than a year, but that was more than enough. It got us to America for Christmas.

They had been married for just six months, my father and his American wife, when they decided that we should visit her family—in America. The actual America. As in *Happy Days*, and *Mork & Mindy*, and *Cagney & Lacey*, and *The Monkees*, *Hawaii Five-O*, *The Six Million Dollar Man*, *The Dukes of Hazzard*. America, America. I was sixteen, an only child, and it was the 1970s, and my parents had divorced and I was a latchkey kid who came home from school and watched tv and ate oven-ready dinners: I had long been marinaded in America; I might as well have been American; the only thing I was actually missing was your actual America.

Previously, for every Christmas, we'd been to

visit my father's parents, my grandparents, who lived in a semi in Swindon. My father's American wife's parents lived in Fort Lauderdale, Florida. In a condo. Fort Lauderdale, Florida. For Christmas. In 1979. At the time, we were living in Tooting, south London. It was like being airlifted from black and white into colour tv.

I had made it. Landfall.

America.

They took me out of school—for a month—and we flew in a jumbo jet—my first time on a plane—and we had to extinguish all smoking materials and I got to meet the pilot, who gave me a badge, and we stayed in a Holiday Inn, and there was *nothing* like flying back then and nothing like a Holiday Inn back in Tooting, no indoor pools with palm trees, and piano lounges, and we ate breakfast every morning in a place called Denny's, which served pancakes and bacon and offered refills of coffee, all of which was unheard of in England—the pancakes, the coffee, the refills—and then we went to Disney World and rode endless rides and then on Christmas Day we visited my father's American wife's parents and my father's American wife wore a white bikini and we had a barbecue, ON CHRISTMAS DAY.

Even now I can't really begin to explain what it was like. You'd have to have known England back in the 70s to be able to appreciate it—a time when nothing seemed possible. And you'd have to have known America too, the great imaginary America of the 1960s and 1970s, everyone's America—where anything seemed possible.

But the most incredible thing of all that Christmas—more incredible even than the jumbo or the refills, or Disney World, or my father's American wife's white bikini—was that my father bought me a record. An LP record. He had never bought me a record before and he never bought me one after. He was probably just looking for something that we could easily take back home in the suitcase. But whatever the intention he must have gone to an actual American record store and asked the actual American behind the counter and presumably bought whatever he was told to buy. He had absolutely no interest in music, my father, so things could have been very different. He might have been advised to buy me *Tusk* by Fleetwood Mac or *The Wall* by Pink Floyd, two of the big albums of 1979. Or Queen, *Live Killers*. But he didn't. By sheer good fortune, the album the American in the American record store in Fort Lauderdale, Florida advised my father to buy me at Christmas in 1979 was *London Calling* by The Clash.

So, there we were, sitting out, four or five thousand miles from Tooting, south London, and my father's second wife is wearing a white bikini and smoking long American cigarettes and mixing drinks and her parents are wearing sports casual wear and they are sleek and tanned and confident in a way that no English person can ever be sleek and tanned and confident, not even now, and my father's American wife's father pulls out this enormous brown hi-fi on a kind of trolley—like a bucking bronco—and he says 'Well, let's give this disc a spin' and he takes *London Calling* and he looks at that photo on the cover of Paul Simonon smashing his bass guitar and he says 'Well, what the heck?' and then he takes the record with his big fat brown American fingers and sets it on the turntable.

The opening song of *London Calling*, as everybody knows, is the best opening song of any record, ever. There's the marching sound of the guitar and the drums and then Paul Simonon leaps in, and then Joe Strummer starts singing and you know—everybody knows—that something is happening here and you don't know what it is, do you Mr Jones, and my father's American wife's father says 'What is this?' And somehow I knew exactly what it was.

It was what people used to call a Polaroid moment. A moment that you wanted to stop and record and share: Fort Lauderdale, Florida, Christmas 1979.

In Fort Lauderdale, Florida, Christmas 1979 it was customary to serve your barbecue with something called a seven layer salad—which is a salad that consists of layers of iceberg lettuce and tomatoes and cucumbers and onions and peas and hard boiled eggs and cheese and bacon, all topped with thick mayonnaise and served in a vast glass bowl, like a trifle, and this was not the sort of salad I was used to back in Tooting. In Tooting we did not eat salads that looked like trifles. Indeed, in Tooting I don't think we had ever eaten a salad at all. And we certainly hadn't eaten a trifle since my father divorced my mother. My mother loved to cook: my father's American wife did not like to cook. My father's American wife did not have time to cook. My father's American wife was always busy with everything. There was always something else going on. Something more glamorous. Something more fabulous. Something more ... American. When they got married and she moved in, all she brought with her were her clothes— lots of clothes—a microwave, and Carlos Castaneda in paperback. As far as I knew no one in Tooting had a microwave in 1979.

'Salad?' asked my father's American wife, between drags on her long American cigarette.

'Dr Pepper?' asked my father's American wife's father.

'Sure,' I said, 'sure' being what my father had started saying to his American wife's every question and request, with a slight American drawl, I had noticed, unconsciously mimicking her. In 'Brand New Cadillac' Joe Strummer sings with exactly the same American drawl—exactly the same. My father's American wife's father had started telling me something about the superiority of American over Japanese cars when my father's American wife asks 'What is this?' and my father says, 'It's the album I bought for him for Christmas.'

'*We* bought for him,' she corrects him, and then she kisses him, and he says 'Sure', although I know

9

and he knows and she knows that it was him and only him that bought me the record, though I can perfectly understand now, looking back, that a woman in a white bikini kissing you on Christmas Day would make just about any man agree to anything. Sure.

Then Joe Strummer yells 'Jesus Christ! Where'd you get that Cadillac' and my father's second wife's mother says 'Is this really suitable, Chip? On Christmas Day?' But before an argument can begin between Chip and Candace—which were their real names, real American names—there are the swingy opening bars of 'Jimmy Jazz' and there's the sound of whistling, like Otis Redding is sitting on the dock of the bay, and my father's second wife's father says 'This is more like it' and he dishes me up some barbecued ribs.

I had never eaten ribs before. I don't think I even knew what ribs were. I had certainly never eaten ribs done on a barbecue before—that sweet, thick taste of barbecued ribs. And I don't think I have ever tasted anything quite like them since. Maybe it was the barbecue sauce. Maybe there was something special about the barbecue sauce available in Fort Lauderdale, Florida at Christmas 1979. Maybe. Maybe not.

Either way, with 'Hateful' my father's American wife began swinging her hips in her white bikini and clapping her hands like a senorita dancing a flamenco and my father was watching her, I remember, with great intensity and I remember he was watching her with that same intensity one night back home in London. I had returned home having been out at a friend's—this was soon after they were married—and they had clearly both been drinking and there was a strange smell in the house, a smell that I realised years later was the smell of weed and I opened the living room door and the two of them were sitting there just staring at each other, intense, but as if in a dream. They were stoned. It was much worse than finding them making love.

The next song I remember off the album is 'Guns of Brixton'—which of course now sounds prophetic. My father was a lecturer in sociology at the old North London Polytechnic and he was there on the march when Blair Peach was killed in 1979, and then there was Thatcher and the Brixton riots and everything else and he became increasingly disillusioned and dissatisfied with mainstream politics and he joined the Socialist Workers' Party and that for us was the 1980s, and that was the marriages gone. I have no memory of us listening to 'Guns of Brixton' that Christmas— the memory has been obliterated by all that miserable future.

But with the next song the memories come flooding back again—'Wrong 'Em Boyo', with that shambling false intro that suddenly segues into a kind of up-tempo two-step and 'This is great!' says my father's second wife and she and her mother start dancing a kind of hoe-down, linking arms and dancing off into the kitchen to fetch more buns for the burgers.

And then there's 'Death or Glory', and my father's second wife's father starts telling me about his time in Vietnam, and 'Koka Kola', and everyone is appalled by the lyrics about 'Coca Cola, Advertising and Cocaine', and 'Lover's Rock' and 'Four Horsemen' and 'I'm Not Down', with its terrible harmonies, and 'Revolution Rock' and then finally we get to 'Train in Vain' and what I remember most vividly of all: my father and his second wife dancing cheek to cheek, in Fort Lauderdale, Florida, on Christmas Day 1979.

It was, without doubt, the happiest day of my life.

And within six months she had gone. She just left. Packed a bag and went, leaving us, me and my dad, with The Clash, the microwave, Carlos Castaneda, and America.

3 DECEMBER

The Sound of a Bag of Carlite Finish

This year I went to eleven funerals. Almost one a month. Mostly the expected, though there was the younger brother of an old schoolfriend. That was unexpected—the younger generation catching up.

A long time ago, when I was a young man —this was when I was working as a labourer—I was working with this plasterer, Roy. He was a real grafter. Plasterers are a different breed. They are not the same as you and me. You have to have something a little bit wrong with you, you've got to be a little bit ... special, to be a plasterer. It's not a trade for lightweights. Total focus, to be a plasterer.

It was coming up to Christmas and of course everyone wants everything done for Christmas, and this fella Roy he had thirteen children—north Belfast—and so he was working flat out, seven days a week, and every penny was accounted for, and he was pushing himself like there was no tomorrow.

And I heard this sound from upstairs—it was a

refurbishment, big old house on the Antrim Road and it was a filthy day, freezing cold, the rain, and the wind off the lough—and I thought at first it was maybe a bag of Carlite Finish, this heavy sound of something solid hitting the floor in this big empty house. And I called out to Roy but there was no reply and so I raced up the stairs and there he was. The first coat of bonding was still setting.

His face was white with dust and the bonding on the wall was all scarred, like rivers, or like veins running across the walls. I remember thinking how his boots were so clean. I always admired the way he kept his boots clean.

I rang the ambulance. And then I rang our boss and then Roy's wife arrived and so there was me and Roy and his wife and the ambulance men, and Roy's wife is crying and saying to me, 'But what am I going to tell the children?' I wasn't much more than a child myself at the time. I didn't know what to say. I felt bad for her and the children.

Most of them did alright. One of the boys went off the rails, but—caught with two Russian grenades and a pipe bomb on the outskirts of Dungannon, but this was way back now during the Troubles. I don't know what happened after. Out on licence with all the others I suppose. I never heard anything else about him.

But the sound. You never forget the sound.

Whenever they drop the body in the ground, or whenever there was an incident, to me, that was the sound—the sound of a bag of Carlite Finish hitting the floor in a big empty house in winter.

4 DECEMBER

Two Words

To All Parents,

It is almost Christmas! We have had a wonderful term, and I would like to thank everyone for their support. It's always a big change for the children coming to school but they have all made the transition very well and you'll be delighted to hear that everyone is now settled in. I just wanted to raise a couple of issues before the end of term. In my experience it's better to get things straight now, so that there are no misunderstandings in future.

So, just a couple of words regarding Christmas. Gift certificates. And another couple of words: hand made. Oh, and another couple: Yankee candles.

Now, to begin with the Yankee candles. Let me be absolutely clear: no. Just no. And before you ask, not even Christmas Pudding? No. Christmas Tree? No. Christmas Anything? No. Ocean Blossom? No. Midsummer's Night? No. French Vanilla? Vanilla Lime? Vanilla anything? No. No. No. No. No. I do not want any kind of scented candle. Or unscented candle. No candles. None. Or perfume. In case you hadn't noticed at the parents' evening, I am a man. Flowers, also no, and vases, absolutely not. Chocolates: have you ever met an underweight primary school teacher, male or female? No, you have not. Novelty mug? Have you ever been in a school staff room? Do you have any idea how many novelty mug cupboards we currently have up and running? And we can't give them away, obviously, in case they turn up in the charity shops from whence many of them doubtless came, so once a year one of us has to go to the dump with boxes full of them. *Boxes*. Of *useless* novelty mugs. Think about it. This is the future of planet Earth we're talking about here, people. You're parents, for goodness sake. You don't need me to remind you, surely?

So what I'm saying is: please consider your Christmas gifts very carefully. Novelty anythings are a bad idea: like all of us, they are destined for landfill. And just for the record, we mostly use laptops and electronic whiteboards these days, so no notebooks, thank you, particularly if they are hand-stitched by orphans—our drawers are full of hand-stitched orphan notebooks. And pens? I would probably consider a Mont Blanc, but otherwise, no. And as for your gift-with-purchase sample cosmetics? Really? Oh, oh—and let me just say it again—I am a man.

This is significant because when I say 'No gift certificates' I don't want you to think that I would refuse all and every gift certificate. It's just that I do not want a facial, for example. Even though I am a primary school teacher—I cannot emphasise this enough—I am a man. I do not want a facial. I do not need a facial. Nor do I want a 20% off voucher for a Christmas hamper. I do not need a Christmas hamper. I am twenty-seven years old and I am a primary school teacher. I am not in a nursing home. If you would consider giving the gift you are considering giving to me to your grandmother, then it is not appropriate. I do not do jigsaws. Or Sudoku. And we are not allowed to accept whiskey, alas.

And as for hand made, just in case I haven't been absolutely clear, ask yourself this question: if you or your child made that thing and you gave it to a complete stranger, would they want it? Unless you or your son or daughter are in fact a professional jeweller, baker or potter—or Kirstie Allsop—please do not give gifts of jewellery, baked goods, or pots. Admittedly, I make an exception for homemade fudge.

Let me say again that it has been a pleasure teaching your children this term and I look forward to seeing them next year.

Happy Christmas.

5 DECEMBER

Just My Job

This is what happens.

I wake up every Friday with a headache.

I take some ibuprofen, the recommended dose.

This doesn't shift the headache. The headache lasts all day.

When I get home I take double or triple the recommended dose, drink a bottle of wine, and three or four large glasses of whiskey. This seems to do the trick.

I have had the Friday headache now for fifteen years.

Sometimes it makes me angry and sometimes it makes me sad.

It will not go away. It is always worse in the winter and at its very worst coming up to Christmas.

Eventually I go to see my doctor. He asks me about my job. I explain about my job. The doctor asks if I think there's perhaps a connection between the headaches and my job. I say no. It's just my job. I can't see that there's any connection between my headaches and the job. My doctor puts me on the waiting list for a course in Cognitive Behavioural Therapy. He says the waiting list is twelve months.

I just need to make it to next Christmas.

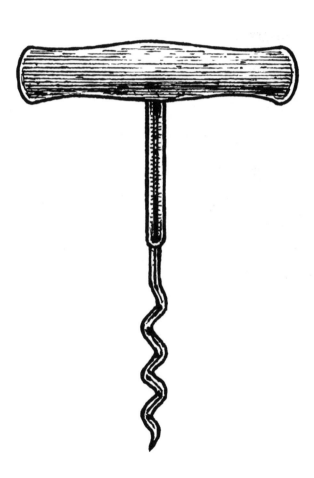

6 DECEMBER

from Sansom's Lives of the Saints:
Saint Nicholas

St Nicholas was a trustafarian. He had dreadlocks, a little beard, played the guitar, was educated at Westminster School, had gone to Oxford, studied PPE, hadn't really enjoyed it, had drifted. He was a disappointment, to himself and others. When he was born, according to his mother, he'd stood up on both his feet when they were bathing him one night, and had sung an aria from Puccini. He was speaking in full sentences when he was a year old. His parents thought they had a genius on their hands. They'd hired a private tutor. He'd learnt languages, instruments. No expense had been spared. But he'd burned himself out. He was searching for a role in life.

His friend had set up a club in Chelsea. A wine bar. St Nicholas had met a girl there. She had two sisters. They were gorgeous. Russian.

It wasn't really a club. It was a clip joint. Men would come in, buy champagne. One thing would lead to another.

It wasn't right. St Nicholas was determined to do something about it.

7 DECEMBER

The Dead White European Male

I am calling my father, to try and make arrangements for Christmas. Making arrangements for Christmas with my father is never straightforward.

When I was young my father was a civil servant. He was normal. Then in his fifties he discovered Buddhism, free love, and communal living. And my mother discovered that he was a total jerk.

Since my mother's death—Crohn's disease, 2012—my father has come to us every Christmas. One year he gave the boys vulture feathers, another year a hand-drawn star map. When the eldest was only five years old, he gave him a bow and arrow, which he had made himself. My wife was appalled. 'I thought he was supposed to be a pacifist,' she said. 'Anarcho-syndicalist,' I corrected her. Last year he brought nothing but taught the boys how to tie knots and braided their hair. My mother was right. He is a total jerk. The boys absolutely love him.

He's not sure if he'll be able to make it for

Christmas. He is busy working on his 'personal dharma memoir'. That's fine, I say. My wife insisted we invite him but if he can't come that's perfect. Win-win.

He has a girlfriend who is younger than me. She's Chinese—he'd prefer it if she was Japanese, but there aren't many Japanese living in Sheffield. She was a waitress, his girlfriend. Her name is something Chinese, but he calls her Tara, after the Buddhist goddess of compassion, which she doesn't seem to mind. Basically, he seems to have found a replacement for the 1950s housewife, which was my mother, but which is no longer available in this country and is available now only on import. Tara wears a lot of heavy red lipstick and wears vintage.

He has quite a cough on the phone. I ask him if he's OK. He says he's fine, nothing that green tea and his herbal remedies can't cure. He is extremely fit. He has the body of a twenty year old, a wild, unkempt holy man beard, and all the physical confidence of someone who spends most of his time outside, growing organic vegetables on his allotment, chopping wood, riding his bike, and going on what he calls walkabouts, which are in fact walking holidays with his Buddhist friends in the Lake District. The rest of the time he studies koans, circulates unfunny emails and drinks malt whiskey. He leaves the housework to Tara.

On the phone he talks to me in the strange, clipped manner that he has long since adopted, refusing to contract verbs, using only the simplest words and syntax. He is talking to me about the depth of time, and how we live in a universe of millions of universes that go on and on and how reincarnation and rebecoming is really all about the deep space within us and outside and the history of the universe within, and I say I have to go and pick up the boys from football.

He says something in Sanskrit—which is how he always begins and ends his phone conversations—and I can imagine him there looking at me, slightly squinting, just as he looked at me as a child, with his pale blue eyes, which my mother always said was what attracted her to him.

And that was the last time we spoke. He died a week later. 'He died at peace,' Tara told me, 'We had made love and he was resting,' which was too much information. 'He was a very generous lover,' she said. Way too much information. 'A very generous man.' At his funeral the boys read a poem they had written for him, comparing him to Father Christmas.

I don't know. Maybe I missed it. Maybe I misjudged him. Maybe I had failed to understand the whole thing. My only consolation of course is that he's maybe coming back round again, so maybe this time I'll get a chance to appreciate him.

At this time of year I find myself looking for him everywhere, but he is nowhere to be found.

8 DECEMBER

Of Course We Do Christmas

Of course we do Christmas. Christmas is important. We live here. I was born here. It's what you do here. People always ask, do you do Christmas? Of course we do Christmas.

We're in the Arndale Centre. My wife is looking for something sparkly. She tries on lots of things and none of them is right but then she finds this red and green dress that's really—it's different. I tell her it makes her look like a Norwegian woodcutter's wife. It really does. There are berries and clasps and all sorts of festive patterns all over it. It gives you a headache just looking at it. But if you like it, I say, fine. And she likes it. She really likes it. So she buys it. She buys also a pair of red boots to wear with it, and a little red shawl. She looks great. It is quite an outfit. You really look the part, I say.

We go for coffee. My wife is drinking a honey and almond hot chocolate and I am drinking a gingerbread latte. We are talking about Christmas dinner—whether we should have the turkey and the brussel sprouts or whether we should think about doing something different. My wife starts humming along with the Christmas carols. She likes Christmas. She likes the Christmas carols. She's in the hospital choir for Christmas—they're singing in the wards. Her favourite is 'Hark! The Herald Angels Sing'. She sings the descant in the choir. She has a beautiful voice.

> Hark! The herald-angels sing
> 'Glory to the newborn King;
> Peace on earth and mercy mild,
> God and sinners reconciled!'
> Joyful all ye nations rise,
> Join the triumph of the skies
> With the angelic host proclaim
> 'Christ is born in Bethlehem'
> *Hark! The herald-angels sing*
> *'Glory to the new-born King.'*

The Qur'an—as you know—does not believe that Jesus is divine. But—as you may not know—it devotes a lot of space to the story of the Virgin Birth, more even—you may be surprised to hear—than the New Testament. The Virgin Birth, according to Islam, is very significant—it is symbolic of the birth of the human spirit. In the Qur'an Jesus is seen as an *ayah*, a revelation of peace but he is not divine. Indeed, in the Qur'an, Jesus denies his divinity and spends a lot of his time attempting to cleanse himself of such blasphemous suggestions.

It's not always easy to explain this to people.

I was born here and I am not religious and have never been religious in any way. But still I struggle to sing the carols. They seem alien to me, inappropriate. My wife, on the other hand, has only lived here for a few years and she loves singing the carols. She loves Christmas. And now she has her special Christmas outfit. She really looks the part.

9 DECEMBER

The Author's Christmas Pudding
(with apologies to Eliza Acton)

50g blanched characters
2 large Bramley cooking plots
200g candied mixed opinions
1 whole style (or 1 tsp grated)
1kg conflict and crises, combined
140g plain language
100g soft fresh white scenes and settings
100g wit, crumbled
3 large free-range sub-plots
1 wineglassful of irony or satire, plus extra to flame
250g backstory, straight from the fridge
Pinch of salt

Mix the ingredients until thoroughly combined and not sticking to the sides. Taste for emotional depth, profundity and high seriousness. Add grammar and punctuation if necessary. Cover and boil in a pudding bowl for two to three and a half years. Decorate with metaphor. Drench in irony or satire—or self-pity if preferred—and set alight. Serve with custard or cream.

10 DECEMBER

Something for Everyone

Kylie Minogue is in a can-can outfit, crawling across a piano.

It was my wife's idea, Christmas treat for the children, down on the train, Christmas shopping, Oxford Street, Regent Street, the lights. They enjoyed it.

And I enjoyed Madame Tussaud's. My Christmas present to myself.

11 DECEMBER

Magnificat/De Profundis

I always thought—I had always assumed—
that there were basically two traditions of painting
the Virgin and Child, and never the twain shall meet.
There is the Italian tradition, which is luminous and
otherworldly and richly symbolic, and there is the
Flemish tradition, which tends to focus on the ordinary
everyday detail. Two distinct traditions. And yet.

Take, for example, Duccio di Buoninsegna's
famous 'Madonna and Child', a classic of the Italian
style, in which the baby Jesus gently pushes away the
beautiful soft folds of the veil of his sad and weary
mother. It's not symbolic or otherworldly: it is a scene
you might see today on the high street. It is a scene of
great pathos. It could be Flemish.

In Joos van Cleve's 'The Virgin and Child',
meanwhile, it looks at first glance as though the
Virgin, mid-feed, has just had a swig of wine, and
eaten half an orange, and is maybe reading the baby
Jesus a bedtime story. But look closer at the sleeping
infant—he looks like a little man, with his feet crossed

and his arms spread. Isn't it in fact a prefiguration of the dead Christ in his mother's arms? A Pietà? And then if you study Mary's reading material, if you look closely, it turns out that it's a prayer book, in which two pages are clearly legible: one shows the Magnificat (Luke 1:54–55), celebrating the Annunciation, and the other De Profundis (Psalm 130:1–2), which is used in the Mass for the dead. It could be Italian.

There aren't two traditions of painting the Virgin and Child. There is only one tradition. There is only one way this story goes.

12 DECEMBER

Thinking of You at ███████ *Christmas*

The only card I received that Christmas was from the police. They thought it was funny. Typical ████████ coppers—excuse my language. 'Thinking of you at Christmas.' That's what got me going to be honest. I thought, I'll ███████ show you—sorry. Thinking of you at ███████ Christmas. They thought that was ███████ hilarious. They'd not had anything on me for years. Years. He was called Coppson, funnily enough, the copper who came up with the Christmas card thing. There was an interview with him in the local paper. 'We want criminals to know we know who they are,' he said. I thought, well, ██████ you Coppson, I want you to know that we know who you are, yeah?

It's not actually that difficult to find out where a copper lives. All you do is hang around the station, wait for them to come out, follow them, and that's it. Couldn't be simpler. It's not like they're working for MI ███████ 5. So I'm hanging around the station, waiting for him to come out and then I follow him back to his house. Nice house, new estate, one of those places with no pavements, garage, nice. I wondered if all his neighbours knew what he did. A lot of people don't like the police.

So the challenge was to come up with something they couldn't trace, yeah? You don't want to get nicked over Christmas. There's nothing ████████ worse than being inside over Christmas. Home cooked brownie's the best you're going to ████████ get at Christmas if you're inside, you know what I mean.

So this is the plan. I go in, Christmas Eve, I'm dressed as Santa. If I'm caught I pretend that someone's put us up to it, it's a surprise for the family.

So I'm in the Santa outfit—big white beard, the red coat, everything. Latex gloves. I ride up in the van, park right outside. No one's going to challenge Father ████████ Christmas, right? And I get in easy through the back door with my Santa sack, two minutes. No ████████ alarm, like he doesn't need it. And I'm loading everything up into the boot of the van and I've taken everything I can find: all the Christmas presents under the tree, plus a laptop, phone, flat screen tv, the usual, and I'm going back in to check for the last few things and I walk into the lounge and there's a little kid sitting on the sofa, eyes wide open, must be his son, four or five years old, and I nearly ████████ jump out of my skin but he's as calm as you like, like it's Christmas yeah, and what else do you expect on Christmas Eve but to find ████████ Santa in your front room, and so he just says Santa? really quiet like, and I nod and I puts my fingers to my lips and I say Shush and I'm turning to walk out and run but he's grabbed my hand and he offers me this little plate of biscuits that he's got all set up ready to give Santa and a little tot of rum and I'll be honest I'm about to give him a little nudge and tell him to ███ off, you know, but he says I've been a good boy Santa, and his eyes are wide open like, and I'm like oh ███, it's ███████ Christmas, I don't know what to say and he says don't tell mummy and daddy I was up before morning and I say all right and he won't let go of my hand and I'm thinking ██████ hell I am ████████.

So me and this little kid end up unloading everything from the van and putting it back in the house—what else could I ███████ do? I'm not a ████████ monster. And then when it's all in this kid produces a big roll of wrapping paper and some ███████ Sellotape and he gives it to me and so I end up wrapping the laptop and the tv and the phone and I am ███████ shitting myself that at any minute Coppson's going to come down and find me with his kid wrapping up his household goods but anyway I get everything wrapped up and then the little kid gives me a Christmas card and a pen and so I write a little note and he gives me a big hug like and I tell him it's time to go back up to bed and off he goes, thank ████.

Thinking of you at Christmas.

They picked me up on Christmas ███████
Day. I hadn't even had my dinner.

My probation officer says if I am honest and tell the story like it actually happened it might help.

13 DECEMBER

Advent

So my mum decided fine, we'd have Christmas early. She wasn't going to have him miss Christmas. She was practical like that. All sorted in a couple of days: the tree, the turkey, everything.

Like they say, dark cloud, silver lining. Best of times, worst of times. Triumph out of adversity.

I wish we could always have Christmas early.

14 DECEMBER

And We Play

Now it's just work. This week alone we've done six shows. Last week we did eight, plus all the school outreach stuff. Next week another six. And then the week after Christmas it's the New Year's concerts.

Frosty the Snowman, The Snowman, Ave Maria with someone from a tv talent show, Sleigh Ride, indoor firework finale. I'm not saying we should be doing Boulez and Schoenberg, but ... It's just about bums on seats these days. You've got to give them what they want.

Most of the people I started with have retired, or moved on, or been paid off. I'm coming up to thirty years. Thirty years up and down to rehearsals, and then the teaching, and concerts at the weekends. When I joined we were still touring: America, Europe. Japan. Shizuoka, the Vienna of Japan they call it, that was something. A full regional symphony orchestra on tour, those days are long gone. They're talking about having to find more than two million pounds in savings next year. It's only a matter of time.

The thing is, I don't know anything else. Picked up the instrument at school, and then uni and auditions and the orchestra. Thirty years. I was going to be Heifetz. I was going to be Stéphane Grappelli.

In the pub afterwards there's a few boys in for a session: guitar, banjo, fiddler. They're not bad. They're OK. 'The Blackthorn Stick'. 'Cliffs of Moher'. 'Star of Munster'. 'Eleanor Plunkett'. The fiddler's his hold too far forward on the shoulder and the wrist up the stick, and it's just this crappy old thing, covered in rosin, but the noise he gets out of it, God, it's powerful.

And of course I've got the fiddle sitting with me. 1971 Dario Verne—nothing special but a good solid instrument, good projection, nice clarity, good range of colour. And between sets they gesture for me to come over.

'D'you want to sit in?'
'No, it's alright.'
'Come on and have a tune.'
'No, it's OK.'
'Come on, it's Christmas.'
'No, no.'
'Come on on.'
'No, no.'
'Give us a tune, big fella, come on.'
'Or what have you got in there? Something you don't want us to see?'
And so I reach down and take it up. And we play.

15 DECEMBER

An Honest Ulsterman

'But why does he do it?' asked my wife.
'I think it's because he's Irish,' I said.
'That doesn't explain it.'
'It explains a lot of it.'

It explained some of it.

The 'it' in question was a poem: my brother-in-law's annual Christmas poem.

He was—he is—Irish, my brother-in-law. *Northern* Irish, he would of course insist. He's always insisting on something. He's an insistent sort of fellow, which is a general characteristic of the Northern Irish—they're renowned for it—but is also a particular characteristic of my brother-in-law, who enjoyed some small amount of fame in the 1970s, which he seems to believe gives him an excuse for insisting on anything and everything, loudly, and in the strongest possible terms. 'An Honest Ulsterman' he signs himself on his Christmas cards, implying both that all other Ulstermen are somehow dishonest, and also that his own honesty is related to an accident of birth rather than to any quality of character. My brother-in-law has absolutely no quality of character.

Suffice it to say that my brother-in-law and I did not—do not—get on. The annual Christmas poem is the only contact we have had for many years. Even that, frankly, is too much.

Back in Belfast in the 1970s my brother-in-law was—apparently—associated with a group of poets who used to meet and read one another's poems in some back room or bar or somewhere and who became known as 'The Group'. 'The Group' happened to include among their number a certain Seamus Heaney, who went on to be awarded the Nobel Prize for Literature and who is—or was—a poet of worldwide renown. My brother-in-law always refers to Mr Heaney either as Seamus—implying a long and continuing friendship, which as far as I know is entirely imagined, my brother-in-law not having been in the same small back room as Mr Heaney for well over forty years—or, occasionally, shaking his head, either in bemusement or delight, as 'The Nobel Laureate'. It's always difficult to tell with my brother-in-law whether he's trying to be witty or menacing—which is another famous trait of the Northern Irish, of course, but also a very particular characteristic of his own.

He left Belfast around the mid-70s, and came over here to work in accountancy, which is where he met my sister, Eleanor, who has been dead now for almost twenty years, alas, while he's still going strong, retired and on a good pension and grown fat with diabetes and gout, and still churning out his bloody poems.

I have kept exactly none of his poems, though I can certainly remember the gist of them. There are basically three or four main themes, which he returns to again and again, like a dog to its vomit, or a sow to its mire. There are poems about Donegal—which my brother-in-law always likes to refer to as his 'true soul landscape', but which as far as I know he hasn't visited since about 1965, much preferring to spend his holidays in France and Italy. And there are poems about his blessed parents, simple peasants who seemed to spend most of their time, according to the poems, digging for peat and potatoes and never uttering anything but proverbs, archaisms, truisms and nary a cross word. His parents were both teachers, in fact—indeed, his father ended up as a headmaster at a famous school in Belfast. I don't know how many peat and potato-digging peasant-teachers there were living in Belfast in the 1950s, perhaps there were some. Perhaps it's poetic licence. There are also the inevitable poems about 'The Troubles', the less said about which the better. And lately, of course, the equally unspeakable poems about peace and reconciliation on what my brother-in-law now insists on referring to always and only as 'the island of Ireland'.

My sister came to us once—it was in the late 1980s. My brother-in-law had been ill-treating her. I won't go into the details. We encouraged her to go to the police and press charges. Instead, after staying with us for a week, she went back to him and we never ever spoke of the matter again. I saw my sister only two or three times subsequently, always in the presence of my brother-in-law, and then, at the age of just 56, on Christmas Eve, more than ten years ago now, she died from cancer. My brother-in-law read a poem at her funeral. I haven't spoken to him since.

So when we receive his annual card with his annual poem, the first week of December, every year, the first card to arrive, I take it carefully from its envelope and place it above the mantelpiece. And there I leave it, with its wise, warm words about the past year and good wishes for the year to come, and whatever poetic sentiments there are about Donegal, and the 1950s, and the Troubles, and the peace process. And then I wait. And I wait. I wait for that moment on Christmas Eve when I allow myself to remember my sister and I roll his letter up tight and I take a match and set light to it and use it as a taper to light the fire.

And then—and only then—do I know that Christmas has truly begun.

16 DECEMBER

The Atheist's Guide to Christmas

Hundreds of people are walking towards a train in a light morning drizzle. They get on the train. Everyone is getting on the train. Some of them realise they have forgotten something. They begin running through the train, towards the rear of the train, but it is too late. The train has departed. There is nowhere to go. There is no going back.

17 DECEMBER

If You Bought the School

Last day of school before Christmas, half day.

'Right, if you bought the school what would you do with it?'

'If I bought the school?'

'If they were selling it.'

'I'd live in it. Do it up a bit. Then live in it. Definitely.'

'How though?'

'I'd put in bedrooms and that. Probably I'd put bedrooms in the maths block.'

'Why?'

'Because it's got a second storey, course.'

'Bedrooms don't have to be second storey. Like in a bungalow, yeah.'

'Yeah, but it'd be good.'

'It's cold, though, maths.'

'Yeah, but. What you'd do, is put in really good heating and stuff in the walls.'

'My aunt had that.'

'Yeah. And I'd have kitchens in A block too.'

'What about the kitchens by the form rooms?'

'You wouldn't want them. They're industrial.'

'Is it just you living in the school then?'

'No, I would live in it while I was doing it up, but then I'd let all my mates in. We'd have a big party.'

'I'd have the hall as like a giant tv room, with a big screen, like a cinema.'

'What about a lounge though? Some sort of chill-out sort of place?'

'There's carpets in English.'

'Yeah. But you can put carpets in anywhere.'

'Music would be good for a lounge. You'd have to get rid of all the whataretheycalled.'

'The partitions.'

'Yeah.'

'You could definitely do it.'

'Shall we do it?'

'Yeah, let's do it.'

Even then, they knew they would never do it.

18 DECEMBER

ORIGINALBEARDEDSANTA.COM

The opportunity presented itself and so I stopped shaving. I stopped shaving on the last day of August. That gave me almost four months. I thought I could do it in four months. But it turns out that it takes more than four months. It takes *years*. It takes a lifetime of commitment. That first Christmas, I'll be honest, it wasn't very good. It wasn't very good at all. The children were a bit disappointed—you could tell. You don't want your Santa with a business-length beard, let alone a stubbly or a moderate or even a merely ordinary beard, even one of those strange shovel-shaped beards that the young people have these days. You want Santa with something really long and thick and huggable— something soft and luxurious, something extraordinary, something beyond the everyday, a big white beard like you get from a dressing-up shop, the kind you see on the Santa in the Coke ads: the real thing. And that sort of beard takes work. It requires dedication. That sort of beard does not just happen. So the following year I didn't shave at all. That was better. But now, now seven years on, my beard, if I say it myself, is absolutely *unrivalled*. I am known throughout East Anglia and beyond as The Original Bearded Santa. There are other Santas available, of course, but there is only one originalbeardedsanta.com. When I started out I used to have to spray it to make it whiter. Now it's white all on its own—nothing added, nothing taken away. There's not a dark hair remaining in my beard: it is guaranteed, all-natural 100% organic and pure pure white.

I used to go to the barber the last week of November but now I go the first week—Christmas comes earlier every year. I usually get my first gig around mid-November—shopping malls mostly. I've been as far south as Dartford and right across to Watford: they all want The Original Bearded Santa. In a good year I can make five or six thousand pounds over Christmas. Every penny goes to charity.

My barber has been trimming the beard for the past few years: it's not a job to do at home with your toenail scissors and your nasal-hair trimmer; tending to the beard of the Original Bearded Santa is a job for a professional. Kaz—Kazim, that's his name—gives it just a light trim, shapes it around the mouth: he understands how to treat a beard. It's because he's Turkish. They understand the culture of beards over there. Kaz himself—who is young, young enough to be my grandson—sports intricate and innovative facial hair. Kaz understands. I trust Kaz implicitly with the beard.

Sometimes the elves ask 'What does your wife think of the beard?' and I tell them of course that she doesn't mind. I don't tell them that I have no wife and that I have never in fact been married, that I live alone and always have. It was a choice. Times were different then. It is not a matter of regret. And now at least, in my old age, I have the beard. The beard is not just a job. It's a vocation. It's my companion.

19 DECEMBER

Around Christmas

We went once a year to the deli. We would drive up to the city and my father—who neither bought nor cooked food for the entire rest of the year—would take us to the deli and he would spend incredible amounts of money on food and on coffee, special dark roast coffee beans, which came in big brown bags stamped 'PRODUCT OF COLOMBIA' and 'PRODUCT OF COSTA RICA'. The coffee would last him all year. He would grind the beans first thing on a Saturday morning and he had a little stovetop espresso pot and he would make himself an espresso and it was the one time in the week when I saw him truly relaxed and happy—with his espresso, and the paper.

In the deli you had to order at the counter and then you took your receipt and you had to pay an old woman who sat in a little booth at the back of the shop, and then you had to go and collect your bags from the counter and we always had so many bags it was like we were travelling with all our worldly possessions.

My father would buy bagels, and salt beef, and chopped liver, and pastrami, and matzo, and matzo meal, and rugelach and babka, and lox and knishes and pickled herring—and gefilte fish. He bought everything. It seemed like everything you could buy in that deli, he bought. And this was a man who bought nothing the rest of the year. But best of all was that when we'd finished shopping in the deli we used to go to *another* deli, just down the road, a different sort of deli, where he would buy cantucci and amaretti and a giant mozzarella, this special mozzarella, it was like a ball, with a twisted knot at the end, like a big white punctuation mark, and the purchase of the mozzarella signalled the end of our annual trip and we were all allowed a little pinch of that mozzarella on the way home, the sweet soft pure taste of fresh mozzarella.

My father was Jewish: my mother was not. My mother was a lapsed Protestant and my father was what you would call fully assimilated. He wasn't just secular: he'd gone all the way. There were no bar mitzvahs, no seder meals—no bris for my brothers—and absolutely no blessing of the Sabbath candles in our house. No mumbo-jumbo. We were brought up entirely without religious education or instruction. The annual trip to the deli was the closest we came to religious observance. It was the only time I ever saw my father with other Jews. It was all Jews in the deli. You knew they were Jews, although they were not Orthodox Jews. They were just ordinary Jews. But there was something about them. There was something about the way my father spoke with them. It was as if something came over him when we entered the deli, and it would last just about until we arrived back home. In the car on the way home he would let us open the box of rugelach and he would sing us a little song, 'Roses are reddish, violets are bluish, if it wasn't for Jesus we'd all be Jewish.' He never spoke to us about being Jewish at any other time. We understood it was not something you talked about.

When we got home with our vast haul of food and coffee my mother would always complain because no one but my father ate any of it—except for the sweet stuff, and definitely not the gefilte fish—and there was nowhere to store it. She would already have done all the shopping for Christmas, and the fridge and the cupboards would be full and there was nowhere to put all his stuff—she always called it his stuff. She didn't like it.

They didn't divorce until we had left home, by which time they had been married for twenty-seven years. 'You serve less time for murder,' my father joked. When they divorced I sided with my mother. We all sided with my mother. My father didn't handle it at all well. By that stage we could all see what it was she didn't like about him. He had always been a rather sad and melancholic man, incapable of expressing emotion or forming close friendships, but when he was younger he at least had his work, which he had always enjoyed. As he grew older he seemed to be incapable of taking pleasure in anything.

'I just needed some fun,' my mother would say whenever I asked her years later about the divorce. She meant everyday fun. She wanted someone to laugh with. Everyone wants someone you can laugh with—and my father was not someone you could easily laugh with. He was born in 1946. 'Too late for them to get me,' he liked to say, which was the closest he ever came to making a joke. Sometimes he would say of his older brothers and sisters, whom he had never met, and of his grandparents and of the rest of his family, apart from his mother and father, who had made it to England, 'Maybe they were the lucky ones.' It always troubled me, even as a child. It troubled me, but it made my mother despair. If there was a single cause for their divorce, I think that was it, it was that one phrase: my father saying 'Maybe they were the lucky ones.'

When my own children were young, around Christmas, I would always try and find time to drive them to a deli where we too would buy bagels, and salt beef, and chopped liver, and pastrami, and matzo, and matzo meal, and rugelach, and babka, and lox and knishes and pickled herring—but not the gefilte fish. It was the best I could do.

20 DECEMBER

BC

BC I worked for a decade in corporate finance. And then earlier this year DH decided it was time to realise his dream of starting his own business, before it was too late, and we agreed that I would do the rest. So just like that I went from WOHM to SAHM and I have to say at first I really enjoyed it. There was so much to do. Things around the home. Little DIY projects. Lunch dates. We got new curtains, I had the floors resanded. DC are day-boarders, so that gives me a little bit of time during the week to myself. (PFB has ASD and a PEP and he's thriving.)

This time of year there's so much to do. Decorations. Presents. The Christmas letter to write, cards, drinks, dinners. Turkey—free-range bronze-feathered. The wine. Crackers—the range of crackers! The tree—we always have a proper tree, RL Norwegian spruce, obvs, but do you go for a Nordmann or a Fraser? DH has no idea. We used to have somebody full-time, now we just have a cleaner. He's started calling me Martha Stewart in front of other people. And he's so busy there's been no DTD for months, though that's a bit of relief TBH.

We used to go away for a bit of warmth. Not this year, obvs. I used to love a bit of langoustine insead of turkey. Anyway, you can't miss it or you'd get bloody depressed—and I should know. Think of what our parents had to put up with.

I know I'm not supposed to say this but FWIW I FHXmas.

21 DECEMBER

Visiting Time

Catherine and the baby went up to her parents for the week. Do you remember? You said you didn't want to come—you wouldn't be good company. We all tried persuading you, but you stood your ground. Do you remember? We'd finished all the paperwork. Sorted the clothes. I took a couple of extra days off work. I couldn't leave you on your own at Christmas.

You hadn't even put up the decorations. 'Your mum used to do all that,' you said. You'd done the cards, though. There were a lot of people who didn't know.

No turkey of course. We had to go and buy one. Turkey crown just—slices. But we had the cake. She'd already done the cakes. One for us, one for sending over to Brian, one for the two of you. You weren't supposed to be eating cake.

On the Christmas Eve I suggested we go for a swim. 'What do we want to go for a swim for?' you said. You used to be a great swimmer. You were very fit. That's what I remember about you when I was a child. How strong you were.

There was hardly anyone there. Christmas Eve. 'It's all changed since the last time I was here,' you said. Unisex changing rooms with cubicles. 'It's not right,' you said. By the time I'd changed and was ready you hadn't even started. I hung around by the showers, waiting. Like being a child again.

Eventually you came out and for a moment I didn't recognise you. The last time we'd been swimming together must have been back when I was about fourteen or fifteen. Was it Devon? I think it was Devon. A real holiday, mum would always call it— do you remember? As in, 'We haven't been on a real holiday in years.'

You didn't have any goggles. You never had any goggles. You climbed slowly down the steps but then you launched straight into your front crawl, just like that. I remember you teaching us front crawl. Three strokes, head to the left, breathe, three strokes, head to the right, breathe. I can only really do breaststroke.

There was music. John Lennon, Slade. I did my usual forty lengths; you maybe did about half.

There were only a few of us in the pool— almost a lane each, and we all got out at around the same time and went to the showers and 'Men and women!' you said. You really didn't approve.

I went into my cubicle and you went into yours. There's a cine film of mum drying me off on a beach somewhere—Wales? I must be about six or seven. The towel looks huge.

And the music was in the changing rooms as well. Bing Crosby, 'White Christmas'. And suddenly this woman's voice joins in, and then another, and then I heard you in your cubicle, in your deep baritone: 'I'm dreaming of a White Christmas. Just like the ones I used to know.' And then I was joining in too, and the tears were running down my face.

And the song came to an end and the voices died away and a man in one of the cubicles says 'Nice one!' and a woman says 'Merry Christmas' and I hear you say, very very quietly, 'Happy Christmas, son'.

Anyway, Catherine is fine. The children are fine. The baby's all grown up now: he's eighteen. And the little one's fifteen. The other one, he's thirteen. That's your grandchildren. We're away to Catherine's parents again for Christmas. They're all fine. They all say hello.

22 DECEMBER

Christmas Bells

The first time I made love to a woman who was not my wife I was sick. It was after. I made my excuses and went to the bathroom. She'd been lying with her arm across me—that was the thing. It wasn't the sex. It was after the sex. Before and during, that was OK, it was good, the adrenaline, the alcohol, everything. But after, her arm lying across me, I was so hot and I was confused. I only just made it to the bathroom. I felt my head against the cool of the toilet rim.

And I remembered as a child one Christmas being sick, with some sort of a fever, and I had received all the presents, and I somehow felt I didn't know what to do with all these presents, and my mother laying me down on cool pillows, and mopping my brow with a flannel and there was nothing to do but to be sick and to recover. I have not had that feeling for many years.

I am in bed with a woman who is not my wife. We have been at a party. Nothing is happening because we have both been drinking and then we shared a joint. Some sort of super-strength skunk and I'm not used to it and I am drifting in and out of sleep and I think I can hear the sound of a car alarm outside and I wonder if it's my car and I get up and go outside and I am standing there in the car park, in the middle of the night and I look up and there are people looking down at me from all the windows up above and the alarm is ringing and I can't turn it off and there is nothing I can do.

23 DECEMBER

*The Busiest People in the Busiest Place
on the Busiest Day of the Year*

He has no luggage to check in.

He buys a toothbrush, socks, a case.

We have to check all the cash and non-cash sales.

★

A man and a woman, the man wearing brogues and those cords that posh people wear. They've bought 2 bottles of gin, a bottle of champagne, 2 paperback John Grishams. The man has dropped the champagne, is claiming he should get a refund 'because it's Christmas'. He says he's a lawyer and he knows his rights. We get the mess cleared up. I tell him to talk to my boss.

★

I am first on the scene. The woman was using

a knife in one of the lounge kitchens. She's lost the tip of her finger. A colleague has put the tip of her finger in an iced Diet Coke. It's quite difficult to find. It's meant to be just ice, I say. I don't think the Diet Coke'll help.

★

A man and a woman, queuing for security. The man is screaming at the woman, who is his girlfriend. Ex-girlfriend? He's white, she's black. I'm black. I'm not listening.

'We had a fucking agreement. No Fucking in the Flat!'

I ask them to quieten down and moderate their language. The man continues shouting. All I'll say is they get a very thorough search and questioning.

★

A man has lost his luggage. He is upset. I am trying to explain.

Here's what happens to your luggage, I say. It has a barcode sticker attached, yes? And it goes on a conveyor belt in a tray, yes? The tray passes several chutes. Each chute for a different flight. And a barcode reader ensures that when it hits the right chute, it tips. Yes? And at the bottom of the chute, a handler checks the bag tag on a computer screen that the passenger has boarded and the luggage then gets loaded. So it might be that the barcode is damaged. Or wrong. Sometimes transfer bags have to be rescreened.

The man doesn't speak English and I don't speak Arabic.

★

A man tries to board the plane. The gate has closed. He's five minutes late. He's drunk. Even then I might have let him board. He can't find his passport. I ask him for his name and he says 'Edward Charles Regina'. I ask him for his address and he says 'Sandringham'. I say, 'Come on, don't piss me about.' He insists that this is his real name. He then pulls out a knife—a tiny plastic knife he must have picked in one of the cafes—and threatens to kill me. I call the police. He'll get five months.

★

A man who looks like Patrick Swayze has taken his shirt off and is shaving in my toilets. I tell him he can shave but he needs to put his shirt on: he can't be shaving with no shirt on in my toilets. He refuses to put his shirt on. I tell him I will have to call the police if he doesn't put his shirt on. 'Fine,' he says, and takes his trousers off. You can't do that in public, I say. You can't take your trousers off in public. 'Well, what about if I do this in public?' he says, and he starts doing something he really shouldn't be doing in

public. People are crazy. I tell my wife. She asks me if
I filmed it on my phone.

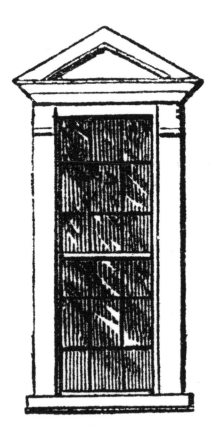

24 DECEMBER

*An Original Period Sash Window
in Perfect Working Order*

An original period sash window in perfect working order. That's what she dreamt of. The perfectly balanced weights, the proportions of it. Cost of repair to include patching in the wood where the old is rotted away, replacing the sash cords, new weights, removing the beading, planing down the sides, an original period sash window in perfect working order, complete overhaul, total cost: £2000. More than a month's wages. But that's what she dreamt of: an original period sash window in perfect working order.

There was nothing in her flat that was in perfect working order. She lived a long way from her elderly parents back home in Ireland. She had not managed to keep up with her friends from school or university. She was not currently in a relationship. She had failed to join any graduate trainee schemes. She was twenty-seven years old, she worked in retail. She was working Christmas Eve. And she was dreaming of an original period sash window in perfect working order.

She dreamt of working somewhere else, of working in a bookshop, in a Waterstones maybe, of coming home at night and reading fresh new novels by contemporary Irish women writers, sitting at the table by her original period sash window in perfect working order. She only needed one. She only needed one special window to forget that she was stuck here with no prospects of any kind. Just one. All the windows in the flat were uPVC except for this one: an original period sash window that needed a complete overhaul and repair, total cost £2000.

She didn't own the flat, of course. She was never going to own a flat. She was renting. The landlord was not going to pay for it to be fixed. But if she could get it fixed she felt that everything would somehow be OK: one original period sash window in perfect working order. It would be her present to herself, her gift to the world. When she had moved on, in years to come, the new tenants in the flat would say a little thank you to the unknown woman, miles away from home, who had given them an original period sash window in perfect working order.

Christmas Eve.

£2000.

She made the call.

25 DECEMBER

Countdown

I don't read women's magazines. Ever. Never. Never have and never will. I am a feminist.

Or what I mean is, I don't *buy* women's magazines.

This is a subtle difference which will be lost on some people, but one which many of my fellow feminists will appreciate and understand, and which makes the reading of women's magazines—under certain very specific circumstances—more or less OK. It works like this. My mother, who is a tiny bit of a feminist, has a neighbour who is most definitely not a feminist who actually buys the magazines and she then passes them on to my mother, who then passes them on to me, so I feel that in some way they have been washed clean by the time they get to me. I feel that I am somehow absolved of responsibility for the content of the magazines. I am merely the end terminus. The receiver. The dead end. The drop. By the time they have reached me the magazines have effectively been rinsed of all harmful bacteria. They are clean. They are kosher. They are more or less edible—like food that has only recently and briefly been dropped on the ground.

As a consequence of this system of exchange—this flow of toxic material down and through generations, becoming slowly sanitised over time, a process which I know many women of a certain age will appreciate and understand—I have quite a collection of women's magazines. In fact, I could probably set up a dentist's waiting room I have so many. The trouble is though, by the time I get them the recipes have all been cut out and the covers are crumpled and the pages are thumbed and they feel dirty, even though both my mother and her neighbour keep their entire houses cleaner than I can keep a single work surface and neither of them have had so much as a cold for years, due to diets which seem to consist mainly of manuka honey, flu jabs and a free-flowing river of NHS antibiotics.

So, I make an exception at Christmas. At Christmas I allow myself to buy a magazine. One or two, for my own private use. I buy the magazine to remind me how to cook Christmas dinner, because every year I seem somehow to have forgotten how to cook Christmas dinner, or perhaps to have half-expected someone else to remember or to offer to do it on my behalf, which they never have and never will. I now have almost two dozen Christmas women's magazines, collected over many years and together, in combination, they have helped me to form my own very personal customised Christmas dinner preparation countdown, which I present to you now in the spirit of sisterhood.

9am: Arrive in the kitchen, hair washed, make-up done, Christmas outfit on. Your outfit should be flattering and comfortable and not so sexy that you have to spend all day fending off your husband/life partner/significant other/relative/family friend who will start drinking early and think that *you* are in some way their Christmas gift. I work on the old 'don't ask for credit as refusal often offends' principle. Even this doesn't always work.

Go to the toilet. You will think that you will have time during the rest of the day to go to the bathroom/bedroom and make yourself presentable but you will not.

Take ibuprofen/paracetamol as appropriate.

Get the turkey out of the fridge. Cover it with a tea towel. A clean tea towel. You'll realise that you do not have enough clean tea towels. Put on a tea towel wash. Remember to take the butter out of the fridge for the bread to go with the smoked salmon and for the brandy butter. You will forget to take out the butter, so return to this step at 10am and 11am when everyone else eventually gets up and decides it's time for smoked salmon but the butter is frozen.

Make a cup of coffee.

Say to your husband/wife/life partner/significant other 'No, it's fine, it's all under control' when they offer to help, because frankly it's easier and anyway what's the point of them offering to help in the kitchen today when they haven't offered to help all year and you really don't want them muscling in on the biggest cooking day of the year and taking some of the credit. Diligently tidy and clean all work surfaces and wonder why on earth you are stuck doing this again, since you've been doing the tidying, cleaning and cooking every day for the past year, even though last year you vowed that this year you weren't going to take on so much at home so you could concentrate more on your job/friendships/personal growth and development. Make a note to speak to your therapist, except you don't have a therapist because you're too busy. Do not have a little cry. At Christmas a little cry always turns into a big cry. Save it.

10am: Remember to turn on the oven. If you have an Aga, well lucky you, bitch. (My sister-in-law has an Aga—which she uses, as is traditional, as an expensive clothes horse.)
Prepare the turkey, gravy and stuffing.
For the stuffing I use a pound of sausage meat, half a pound of chestnuts, herbs, celery and onion but frankly none of it really matters as long as it contains lots of sausage meat—indeed, in extremis you could probably scrap the rest of the dinner and just serve sausages and everyone would be happy.
For the gravy use fresh chicken stock—like you've got fresh chicken stock! Use a stock cube, for God's sake and don't be so bloody precious, plus a dash of white

wine, some dried thyme and a bay leaf, because no one cares or can tell the difference, except your sister-in-law, but when was the last time she made Christmas dinner?

Cram the stuffing in the front cavity of the turkey. Thread a skewer through the folds of skin around the front cavity to keep it all in—try not to be reminded of what this reminds you of. Realise you haven't got a skewer any more because you used them all for something in the garden. Do not staple or use Sellotape, obviously. Improvise. I don't know with what—that's the point of improvisation. But in my experience a sharp pencil works. Not a coloured pencil.

Butter and salt and pepper the turkey. Forget all that stuff about stuffing butter under the skin. Again, try not to think about what handling turkey skin reminds you of. Thank God you're past all that.

10.30am: Put turkey in the oven on a trivet. Realise again that you don't know what a trivet is—then remember that it's that metal rack type thing that comes with your roasting pan that you never use.

Prepare bread sauce: half a white loaf, cubed, onion studded with cloves, 23fl oz milk, bay leaves, pinch of nutmeg, 100ml double cream. Put onion in saucepan with milk and bay leaves and nutmeg. Bring to boil, simmer for 10 mins, leave for 20 minutes. Discard. Nobody actually likes bread sauce.

11am: Baste the turkey with the fat that will already have formed at the bottom of the roasting pan. Do this every half an hour for the next couple of hours, until you realise that you have forgotten to remove the neck and giblets in the plastic bag inside the turkey carcass. When you do eventually realise, remove the neck and giblets from the carcass, and the bag, and put them in the bottom of the roasting pan. Or the bin.

Prepare brandy butter: whisk 150g butter until creamy. Wish you had an electric whisk that worked. Perhaps start to feel a little sad. Do not have a little cry. Under no circumstances have a little cry. Add sugar until light and fluffy. Realise that your whisked butter and sugar are never light and fluffy. Trickle in the brandy. Watch it curdle. Despair. Put in fridge. Realise fridge is full. Leave on windowsill. Buck yourself up, woman. Bucks fizz.

11.30am: Guess what? Baste the turkey. It should be getting a little bit brown. It won't be getting a little bit brown. But the next time you check it'll be too brown, so cover with foil. Scatter chopped carrots, celery and onion over giblets in bottom of the roasting pan.

Prepare vegetables. Six pounds of floury potatoes. Pound of carrots. Two pounds of swedes. Three pounds of brussel sprouts.

If you don't know how to prepare vegetables by now, give up.

12 noon: Realise you forgot to put turkey back in oven. Put turkey back in oven. Turn down heat in oven to 180. Keep bird covered. Put Christmas pudding on plate in a pan. Forget all about it, allowing to burn to

a crisp, as usual.

Prepare first course. Remember that you have forgotten to plan the first course. Make do with the leftover smoked salmon. Cut bread in triangles. It'll do.

12.30pm: Pour off fat in turkey tray, save in bowl, leave giblets and mushy vegetables in tray, crumble stock cube, add white wine, thyme, bay leaf. Return to oven.

Finally give in to demands that presents be opened. Wander in and out of the kitchen as people pretend to know what they've bought each other, since in fact you've bought all the presents for everyone, from everyone. Smile weakly. Look serene. Need I say that when you realise that your husband/wife/life partner/ significant other actually believed you when you said you shouldn't do presents for each other this year and so they actually haven't got you a present—do not cry.

1.30pm: Boil potatoes.

Look for jar of cranberry sauce. You're sure you bought cranberry sauce. But maybe that was last year. Or the year before. The year before that? Realise that time is running out and that you are another year older than the last time you were hunting for cranberry sauce. Ignore sister-in-law who says she always likes to make her own cranberry sauce. Pity her. She's married to your brother.

1.45pm: Take turkey out of oven. Keep it covered in foil. Realise you have run out of foil. Improvise.

Perhaps use your sister-in-law's coat? Dismiss the thought from your mind.

Raise oven temperature back up to max. Put potatoes in oven.

2.15pm: Don't touch the potatoes. Seriously, don't touch. They'll be better if you don't touch them. Alright, go ahead, touch them. They will not get crispy if you touch them, but you're going to touch them anyway, so touch them.

Mash carrots and swedes. Wish you had a mouli-legumes. Add butter, pepper, salt, whatever, anything. Told you you shouldn't have touched the potatoes.

Boil sprouts then fry them, desperately, adding bacon, in an attempt to make them taste of something. Fuck the vegetarians.

Take the turkey tray, make gravy, blah, blah.

Serve it. Look at it. Look at them.

Before sitting down, make your excuses and go to bathroom.

Look at yourself in the mirror. Do not have a little cry. Put on some lipstick. Smooth your hair. Realise that what you are looking at is the face of your mother.

26 DECEMBER

Phantom Limb

He was walking to the off-licence. His leg was stiff and he needed the fresh air. Clear his head.

They'd been drinking since eleven. Few friends. The tenners in his pocket bulging, plenty of money to spend on top-ups. Beer, definitely. Spirits? Something special for the ladies? Baileys or something, seeing as it was Christmas? Wine?

No. Wine? Stick with vodka. Vodka and a few fags. Everyone's on the e-cigs these days. But it's Christmas. Vodka, fags. And snacks. Pringles, yeah? You can't drink on an empty stomach.

The day his dad retired from the post people had him in for drinks—sherry, wine, beer, whatever. All sorts. His dad knew everyone on his round by name. Different world. He got so drunk he was sick, eleven o'clock in the morning. He'd never been drunk in his life before, virtually teetotal. Someone called the office and they came and put his bike in the back of the van and drove him home. The next day he was totally ashamed.

He hasn't been in work for five years. He's on DLA.

Everything had changed. The shops were all open. Used to be shut up on Boxing Day, didn't it? Apart from the big stores up on Oxford Street. It's not like Christmas used to be. Veiled women, the bearded men. What used to be the old Co-Op has become the Sari Palace. Dewar's the butcher's, that's AfroImports—necklaces, carved wooden stuff. The rest is all take-aways, nail and beauty bars, charity shops. Library's shut. Pub's a Wetherspoon's. The streets are filthy.

He doesn't know anyone anymore. Big family of Poles in the off-licence, never the same person twice. Used to be Mr Woodward. He knew all the Woodwards. One of the boys joined the RAF. He doesn't even know his neighbours now: Chinese on one side of them, Greeks or something on the other.

He gets his wallet out to pay. There's the old half a pound note. Him and his twin brother Terry tore the pound note in half—what, twenty odd years ago now? twenty-five? more?—the night before Terry emigrated to Australia. When we next see each other we'll put that pound together and buy ourselves a drink. He'd never made it over and Terry had never made it back. Why would he? A pound won't buy you a drink now, will it.

Boxing Day they used to have everyone in—
all the neighbours, sharing the leftovers, bit of ham,
bit of cheese and biscuits. And on Christmas Eve his
mother always went to Midnight Mass. The whole
street did. You knew where you were. The woman
he's with at the moment says she's a Buddhist. She's
alright though. Quarter Jamaican. He's London Irish.
England for the football and the Olympics, Ireland for
the boxing.

He's broadminded. He's not even UKIP. He
used to be Conservative but now he's nothing. His
MP came round a few years ago, campaigning at the
last election, and he knocked on the door and he let
the MP say his piece and then he started asking about
all the immigrants coming here and taking over and
taking our jobs and the MP yawned and that was it,
that tells you everything, doesn't it? That's all you need
to know. He hasn't voted since.

He was a brickie before, even had a job in Berlin
after the fall of the Wall. Rebuilding civilization, wasn't
it. Happy days. But after the accident, and now with all
the changes, and he gets these stabbing pains. Phantom
limb, they call it. The drink helps. It's medicinal.

27 DECEMBER

I Do Not Like It
(But I Am Not Paid To Like It)

I was brought into the boardroom. Boardrooms are usually used for board meetings, obviously. The boardroom is the ultimate expression of the power of a business. It is the high altar of commerce. In the boardroom everything is official and formal—it is a place of ritual and ceremony.

When I walked in there was a man with his feet up on the table. And there was another man munching an apple. A table tennis net set up on the table—a hard black polished table. And another man lying on the table. CEO. CTO. CFO. They're all in black T-shirts and jeans. Usual corporate trophies on the wall: framed magazine covers; first editions of advertising runs; certificates of entry from the NASDAQ; the cover of the first technical manual.

The CEO is the man lying on the table.
'We like you,' he says.
'Yes, we like you,' says the man munching the apple, the CTO.

'We like you a lot,' says the man with his feet on the table, CFO.

They were offering me to head up their Information Department. My own team, own staff. Eyes and ears of the company. I was Head of Operations elsewhere, at a competitor. I'd started out as an engineer. Details. I'm into the details. I asked about the job description. There was no job description. I was to be responsible for everything and anything that happened inside or outside the walls of the company.

'So what do you want?' asked the CEO.
'I'm not sure,' I said.
'We're offering 250 plus stock,' said the CFO.
'I'll have to think about it,' I said.
'350 and we'll double the size of your options if you don't have to think about it.'
'And if I have to think about it?'
'Are you going to take the position or not?'
'I need some time to think about it.'
'This,' said the CTO, tossing his apple core into the bin, 'is your time. Up.'
'I'm in,' I said.
'Immediate start,' said the CEO.
'Fine,' I said.
'I mean like, now,' said the CEO.

I was briefed on the way out. Everything was set up—swipe cards, codes. Lift going down, down to the floor with all the engineers. My people. Doors opening. Best way is to get it over and done with.

'Ladies and gentlemen,' I say. 'I'm afraid I have some bad news.'

So that was my Christmas. How was yours?

28 DECEMBER

Downtime

I was going to be an artist. I was always going to be an artist. But I wasn't allowed to go to college. This was the late 50s. I used to go to the dances at the art college. Boys in jeans. You'd never seen anything like it. Then I joined the Socialist Labour League. CND. We shall not be moved. I met him on the Aldermaston marches. That was what '59, '60? And then it was the early 60s and we were listening to Charlie Mingus and Sonny Rollins and that's when we started the drugs. Tea, he called it.

He called himself a tea importer and exporter. He'd get these 40 kilo shipments of kif from Morocco and then he'd sell it at £4 an ounce. We had a little car, we'd drive up to Tilbury, collect the package, sell it on. Very straightforward. Ten-bob deals, wrapped in newspaper. Jamaican grass, third of an ounce, that was cheap. And we used to sell some ready rolled—French cigarettes we called them. I was so naive then. I thought I was Jean Seberg. We had a house in St John's Wood. It didn't bother me. I didn't really know anything about drugs, apart from the fact that some were brown and some were white, some you smoked, others you didn't, I didn't ask, that was it, and that was it, except when we started to branch out. Straight coke or expensive coke that had amphetamines in, and then the heroin. It started to get complicated. He disappeared.

We haven't seen each other for years. He was just in town, he says. He's staying in some sort of boutique hotel in Soho. Must have done alright for himself. Cleaned up his act. How about a drink, for old times' sake, in that downtime between Christmas and New Year?

He's drinking mineral water and wearing a trilby, Ray-Bans, a silk scarf, black jeans, and exactly the same expression he was wearing the last time I saw him, only it doesn't look as good on him now. This man, who used to look like Bob Dylan or Keith Richards, now he looks like a man dressed up as Bob Dylan or Keith Richards. With Botox. And I can tell he's bald, under the hat. And he's wearing dark glasses. I used to have a little job as a journalist—features, celebrity interviews. I had to go round to their hotels and talk to these people. They were all the same. You'd eat lunch with them, write something about them. Absolutely no self-knowledge. I hated doing it.

He's already ordered my drink—I used to drink Pernod. It's funny that he's remembered. I haven't drunk Pernod for years.

'You haven't spiked my drink?' I say, as I sit down.

'Come on,' he says. We kiss. 'You look great,' he says. I've had a little bit of work done myself. Hair done. Make-up. Gave up smoking. Been using the same face cream for forty years. Not exactly a size 8 anymore. But I tell you what: I may not look great but I look a hell of a lot better than him.

I ask him about his family—I'd heard he'd got married, had children, divorced, the usual. He asks me about mine. Husband dead, children. Cats. He's not listening.

And then he tells me this story about how he was sitting in some restaurant in Kuala Lumpur—KL, he calls it—and he realised that he needed to reconnect with his past, back home in England, the people who were important to him, some old spiel, and then he says isn't it funny that we're both free agents again now and how this time of year can be lonely without anyone to look after you, and he asks if I'd like to freshen up upstairs in his room. Fortunately I am way past all that and I certainly don't need anyone to look after. So I decide to go shopping instead. I tell him it was nice to see him but I think he's looking for a younger woman, and good luck. He can pay for the drinks.

I walk down St Martin's Lane to Trafalgar Square—my boots are killing me. I go straight to the artists' supply place down by the National Portrait

Gallery. I haven't painted for years. I used to do a few little craft things. Every year I'd make something special for the grandchildren. Small things. Doll's clothes. PE bags. I buy a small easel, some oils, brushes, and I get a cab home.

I don't have long. When I get home it's not too late.

29 DECEMBER

Cellophanitis

My mother died of cellophanitis. She didn't, in fact. There is no such disease as cellophanitis, as far as I'm aware. She died of lung cancer. But we like to joke that she died of cellophanitis because she always used so much cellophane. Eight of us to feed. After she died we found ancient foodstuffs in her fridge which had been embalmed in cellophane—as if by mummifying her cheese she might somehow save herself.

So as we're wrapping up the remains of the leftovers we're talking about mum and we're talking about the cellophane. She used it on the windows also, says my sister—to keep out the draughts. I'd forgotten. To keep out the draughts. To keep in the freshness.

30 DECEMBER

A Very Exotic Juice

We saved for ten years. Ten years. We wanted to treat the grandchildren. We weren't sure what we were going to treat them to, but then we saw a holiday programme and that was that. He got it in his head. Take everyone away at Christmas to a foreign hotel. Luxury, mind. Eight hundred rooms, six restaurants, boutiques, a spa, kids' camp, night club, waterpark. Everything in one place.

Charter flight, bus to the hotel. Greeted with little cups of juice and fruit. All very nice. The lobby was vast. Marble, marble staircases. Identifying wristbands. Attendants with walkie talkies. Big walls, gates. Totally secure.

The first day me and my daughter had a seaweed wrap and a salt scrub in the spa—beautiful. The boys sat by the pool. Drinks all inclusive. The only trouble was the children hated the kids' camp and refused to go back the next day. Mostly Russians.

Cleaners at it the whole time. People would

throw rubbish anywhere, expecting someone to pick it up—and they did.

The food! All-day ice-cream bar. All-day bar. Big buffet: pasta, steak, tapas, lobster. And the desserts: tiramisu, cheesecake. 'If I lived here I'd explode,' I said.

And then we had to leave. We had to pack up quickly and leave. And as we were leaving I noticed this charge on the bill. I'm the one who's always kept an eye on the bills.

'What's that for?' I ask the woman. She's hurrying us on the bus.
'Everyone has to go,' she says.
'I'm going,' I say, 'but what's that for?'
She looks at the bill.
'Resort fee,' she says.
'Resort fee? What's the resort fee?'
'For the welcome,' she says.
'The welcome?'
'The welcome and the juice.'
'For a welcome and a glass of juice, I have to pay how much?'
'Madame,' she says, 'It is a very exotic juice.'

31 DECEMBER

Auld Lang Syne

She neatly arranged the fish bones, skin and almonds on the plate, so that the waitress wouldn't think she was messy. They skipped dessert. The coffees came. A glass of dessert wine, perhaps? They shouldn't, but they did.

Midnight came. Auld Lang Syne. There was a band but they weren't in the mood for the band. On the way upstairs, she pressed her lips to his cheeks.

'Thank you,' she said.

'Goodnight,' he said.

He cried himself to sleep, the tears running down into his ears and fizzing around inside his head.

In the room opposite, she lay on the bed fully clothed, exhausted. The wash basin gurgled, there was the sound of laughter from the corridor. Someone pacing around upstairs. And what was that? Fireworks outside? People only used to have fireworks on Guy Fawkes night, but they were everywhere these days.

She did not cry. She had cried herself dry the past year and had no more tears to shed.

At breakfast they were all smiles again.

'How'd you sleep?'
'Fine. Lovely. Nice firm bed.'
'Good.'

And then the breakfasts came.

'I'll never eat all this, not after last night.'
They ate in silence for a while.
'Your dad loved a good cooked breakfast.'
'Yes, he did.'

They ate the rest of the meal in silence.

She wished she'd had more children.

He wished he'd married.

Then they went up to their rooms and packed up their few bits and pieces.

It was his idea to take her away for New Year. He couldn't bear the thought of visiting her at home. Or her coming to him, to his flat. No spare room and he only has the futon in the lounge. She doesn't feel comfortable at his.

But he can't go to her. Her house doesn't feel like home anymore. Two years ago they'd had it all fitted out. Stair lift. Grab rail. Emergency cord. Metal framed commodes. Cheap, horrible stuff. She still had it all everywhere, like a reminder and ready for her now: waterproof pants and incontinence pads; that stick thing to dress with; button hook; jar opener; the board to hook over the edge of the table.

So he drove her home and then he drove himself home.

All of his friends were married. It was difficult to remain friends with people once they were married and had children. Their lives changed. There was a woman at work. They joked sometimes about getting together. She wasn't his type but maybe it didn't matter. Friends just, acquaintances. Companions. Maybe this year.

ACKNOWLEDGEMENTS

For previous acknowledgements see *The Truth About Babies* (Granta Books, 2002), *Ring Road* (Fourth Estate, 2004), *The Mobile Library: The Case of the Missing Books* (Harper Perennial, 2006), *The Mobile Library: Mr Dixon Disappears* (Harper Perennial, 2007), *The Mobile Library: The Delegates' Choice* (Harper Perennial, 2008), *The Mobile Library: The Bad Book Affair* (Harper Perennial, 2010), *Paper: An Elegy* (Fourth Estate, 2012), *The Norfolk Mystery* (2013), *Death in Devon* (2015), *Westmorland Alone* (2016) and *Essex Poison* (2017). These stand, with exceptions. In addition I would like to thank the following. (The previous terms and conditions apply: some of them are dead; most of them are strangers; the famous are not friends; none of them bears any responsibility.)

50 Watts, Kobo Abe, Giorgio Agamben, Brian Aldiss, Ali al-Du'aji, Haifaa al-Mansour, Wes Anderson, A-WA, Richard Ayoade, Jean-Michel Basquiat, the Blind Boys of Alabama, Michael Bond, Anthony Bourdain, Lili Brik, the Brisley Bell, Build an Ark, CB Editions, Cabinet Magazine, Orly Castel-Bloom, Beth Chatto, Jeremy Clarke, Joshua Cohen, Stephen Connolly, Mike Coupe, Dalkey Archive Press, Frédéric Dard, Liz Dawn, the Dial House, the Doobie Brothers, Danny Dreyer, Ross Edgley, Elmham Surgery, Equiknoxx, Mohammed Fairouz, Chet Faker, *Fauda*, Simone Giertz, Natalia Ginzburg, Emma Goldman, Michel Gondry, Gramatik, Ayelet Gundar-Goshen, Ed Hands, Jim Harrison, HM

Tower of London, Charlotte Higgins, Hooverphonic, Michael Hughes, Sean Hughes, the Institute of Economic Affairs, Shirley Jackson, Alejandro Jodorowsky, Velly Joonas, the Joubert Singers, Mark Kermode, Sam Leith, Larry Levan, David Markson, Samar Samir Mezghani, Ferdinand Mount, Ben Myers, Mike Nichols, Martha Nussbaum, Iona Opie, Shelly Oria, Peter Osborne, Lawrence Osborne, Over the Rhine, Nick Parker, Mark Pawson, Tom Petty, Zbigniew Preisner, Dorit Rabinyan, the Railway Tavern, Randomer, Shan Sa, Luc Sante, Ryuichi Sakamoto, Peter Sallis, Habib Selmi, Tony Servillo, Anoushka Shankar, Viktor Shklovsky, Christopher Skaife, Jaz Skaife, Edward Soja, Sons of Kemet, Paolo Sorrentino, Harry Dean Stanton, Swagger, David Torrans, the Ulster Independent Clinic, the University of Reading, Ayelet Tsabari, Emma Warnock, the University of Westminster, Heinz Wolff, the Wolseley, Woodkid, Shifu Yan Lei.

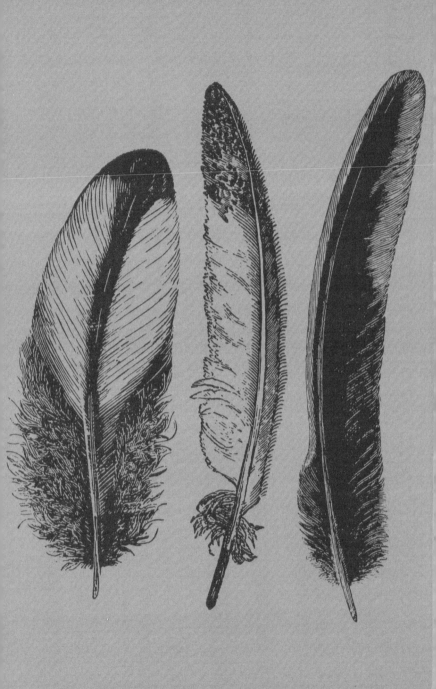